Emma at the Fair

By Margriet Ruurs
Illustrated by Barbara Spurll

Fitzhenry & Whiteside

To Armstrong's Interior Provincial Exhibition, the Fairest of them all
— Margriet

To my dance partner
— Barbara

Text copyright © 2005 by Margriet Ruurs
Illustrations copyright © 2005 by Barbara Spurll

First published in paperback in 2007

Published in Canada by Fitzhenry & Whiteside,
195 Allstate Parkway, Markham, Ontario L3R 4T8

Published in the United States by Fitzhenry & Whiteside,
311 Washington Street, Brighton, Massachusetts 02135

www.fitzhenry.ca   godwit@fitzhenry.ca

10 9 8 7 6 5 4 3 2 1

Library and Archives Canada Cataloguing in Publication
Ruurs, Margriet, 1952-
Emma at the fair / by Margriet Ruurs ; illustrated by Barbara Spurll.
ISBN 978-1-55005-126-1 (bound).-ISBN 978-1-55005-127-8 (pbk.)
I. Spurll, Barbara II. Title.
PS8585.U97E443 2005   jC813'.54   C2005-903735-0

U.S. Publisher Cataloging-in-Publication Data
(Library of Congress Standards)

Ruurs, Margriet.
Emma at the fair / Margriet Ruurs ; illustrated by Barbara Spurll.
[32] p. : ill. col. ; cm.
Summary: An enthusiastic and naive chicken learns what other creatures do
to win a ribbon at the country fair, but she's only willing to be herself.
978-1-55005-126-1 (bound)   978-1-55005-127-8 (pbk.)
1. Chickens - Fiction. 2. Fairs - Fiction. I. Spurll, Barbara, ill. II. Title.
[E] dc22   PZ7.R945Emf 2007

Fitzhenry & Whiteside acknowledges with thanks the Canada Council for the Arts, and
the Ontario Arts Council for their support of our publishing program. We acknowledge the
financial support of the Government of Canada through the Book Publishing Industry
Development Program (BPIDP) for our publishing activities.

Design by Wycliffe Smith
Printed in Hong Kong, China

Emma scurried through wet fall leaves after slow, fat flies. Two magpies laughed at her from the branches of a mountain ash tree.

The farmer was raking leaves, and the musky smell of mushrooms and the sweet scent of apple pie hung in the air.

Emma was scuttling around the corner of the farmhouse when suddenly,

"TOK!"

She came beak to nose with a huge, orange face! Emma scraped the ground and puffed herself up as big and round as a watermelon. But the face staring back at her was bigger and rounder. It had a scary sort of grin.

Then the farmer's children came around the corner, laughing. "Look, Emma, isn't this the most beautiful jack-o'-lantern you ever saw?"

Emma pretended to be stalking a sleepy grasshopper.

Cool as a cantaloupe. She had known all along that the face was just a jack-o'-lantern and nothing to be afraid of.

The farmer's wife came out of the farmhouse carrying a huge jar of pickles. "I'm ready to go to the Fall Fair," she said. "Haven't you put Emma in her cage yet?"

With gentle hands the children scooped Emma up and put her in a small cage. The big, round face seemed to wink at her.

"I sure hope Emma wins a ribbon," said the girl.

"Tok!" said Emma. She didn't know what a ribbon was. And she didn't know how to win one. But if her girl wanted a ribbon, Emma would try her best.

The family piled into the old truck. The farmer's
wife drove. The farmer held the jar
of pickles on his lap.

In the back seat, one of the children held Emma
in her cage; the other one held the big, round,
grinning face on his lap.

Soon they arrived at the Fall Fair and tumbled out of the truck. The farmer wandered over to where huge cows were being brushed and blow-dried. The farmer's wife took her jar of pickles into the Exhibit Area. The boy took the big, round, grinning face to the Produce Barn.

And the farmer's girl carried Emma to the Poultry Barn.

Inside it sounded and smelled like Noah's Ark. Row upon row of cages held gaggles of geese and dozens of ducks. Turkeys and roosters of all sizes made a racket. It was a cacophony of cackles.

The girl put Emma's cage on a table to watch the Rooster Crowing Contest. Each rooster tried to outdo the other with a louder, longer "Cock-a-doodle-doo-hoo-hoo!" Emma had never heard such a ruckus.

The winner received a big red ribbon on his cage.

"See," said the girl to Emma, "that's what I want you to win!"

"Tok!" said Emma. That would be easy. She puffed up her chest, just like the roosters did. She scraped her throat and then she huffed and she puffed and tried to crow as loudly and boisterously as the roosters did. But the only sound that came out was a soft "Tok-a-bokkk!" No matter how hard she tried, she couldn't say cock-a-doodle-doo.

Next they watched the turkey judging. Each proud turkey strutted his stuff, flaunted his feathers, and gobble-de-gob-bled as loudly as he could. Emma had never heard such a brouhaha. The biggest, fattest, loudest turkey received a bright blue ribbon on his cage.

"See," said the girl to Emma, "that's what I want you to win!"

"Tok!" said Emma. Now that would be easy. Emma shook out her tail and fluffed up her feathers. She tried strutting up and down like the turkeys, but her cage was too small. She hit her head on the top and tripped over her toes. No matter how hard she tried to gobble-de-gobble and flaunt, the judges didn't even notice Emma.

Then they announced the pigeon-plop. People anxiously crowded around. Emma strained her neck to see pigeons parading in a special cage with large bingo numbers on the floor. They pranced and promenaded and they ookerookooed. There was great excitement when one of the pigeons dropped a plop on a number on the floor. The ticket holder with that number won a prize and the pigeon won a gorgeous green ribbon on her cage. Emma had never seen such prancing.

"See," said the girl to Emma, "that's what I want you to win!"

"Tok," said Emma with her beak in the air. No matter how badly the girl wanted a ribbon, Emma knew that a chicken would not lower herself to be like those pigeons. She sighed and settled down on the straw nest in her cage, like the lid on a cookie jar.

Emma was tired of all this ribbon business. And while the girl went to check out the other chickens, Emma decided to take a nap. First she laid a perfect egg and then she dozed off to escape all the hustle and bustle.

Suddenly, Emma was wide awake. A judge with a clipboard was staring right at her. Emma puffed up her chest and shook out her tail. Softly she tok-tok-tokked at the judge.

The farmer's children ran back to Emma's cage. The boy was holding the big, orange face. It had a bright blue ribbon on top of its head, and it seemed to wink at Emma.

"That's our chicken!" the girl said proudly. "Emma doesn't cock-a-doodle-doo like the roosters. She doesn't flaunt like the fat turkeys. And she doesn't prance like the pigeons. But Emma lays the best eggs in the world!"

The judge smiled. "That certainly is one of the best-looking chickens I have ever seen!" he said. Then he put a wonderful white ribbon on Emma's cage.

"TOK!" said Emma. She had known that all along.